ISBN-13: 978-1508816041
ISBN-10: 1508816042

MY T-REX HAS A TOOTHACHE
it keeps him up all night!

He moans and groans,
gnaws and roars,
it's such a sorry sight.

MY T-REX
HAS A
TOOTHACHE
it's put
him off his
food!
REX

He won't eat pork chops... Triceratops... Or Anything that's Stewed

MY T-REX HAS A TOOTHACHE!

It Gets worse every DAY!

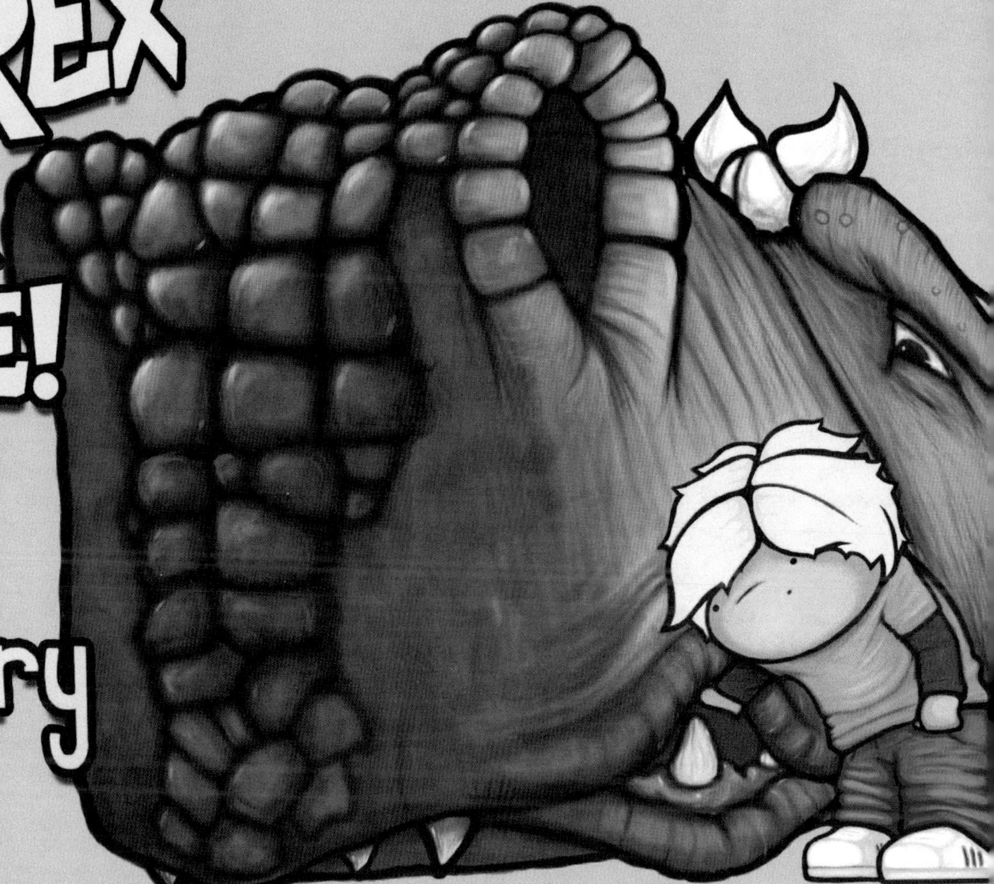

I took him to the Dentist

But the Dentist

ran away!

I took him to my teacher
and asked her what to do!

But she leapt behind her desk and shrieked...
"That thing belongs inside a Zoo!!!"

My T-REX has a toothache...

It's driving him BERSERK!

Aha that's it! I have a plan...
I think it's going to work!

Your gums are red,
your mouth is sore,
you are a
poorly
Dinosaur!

That tooth is loose
there is no
doubt.
So why
dont you...

...Just ROAR it out!

Let the Roarfest Begin!

ROAR! ROAR!!!
and roar some more!

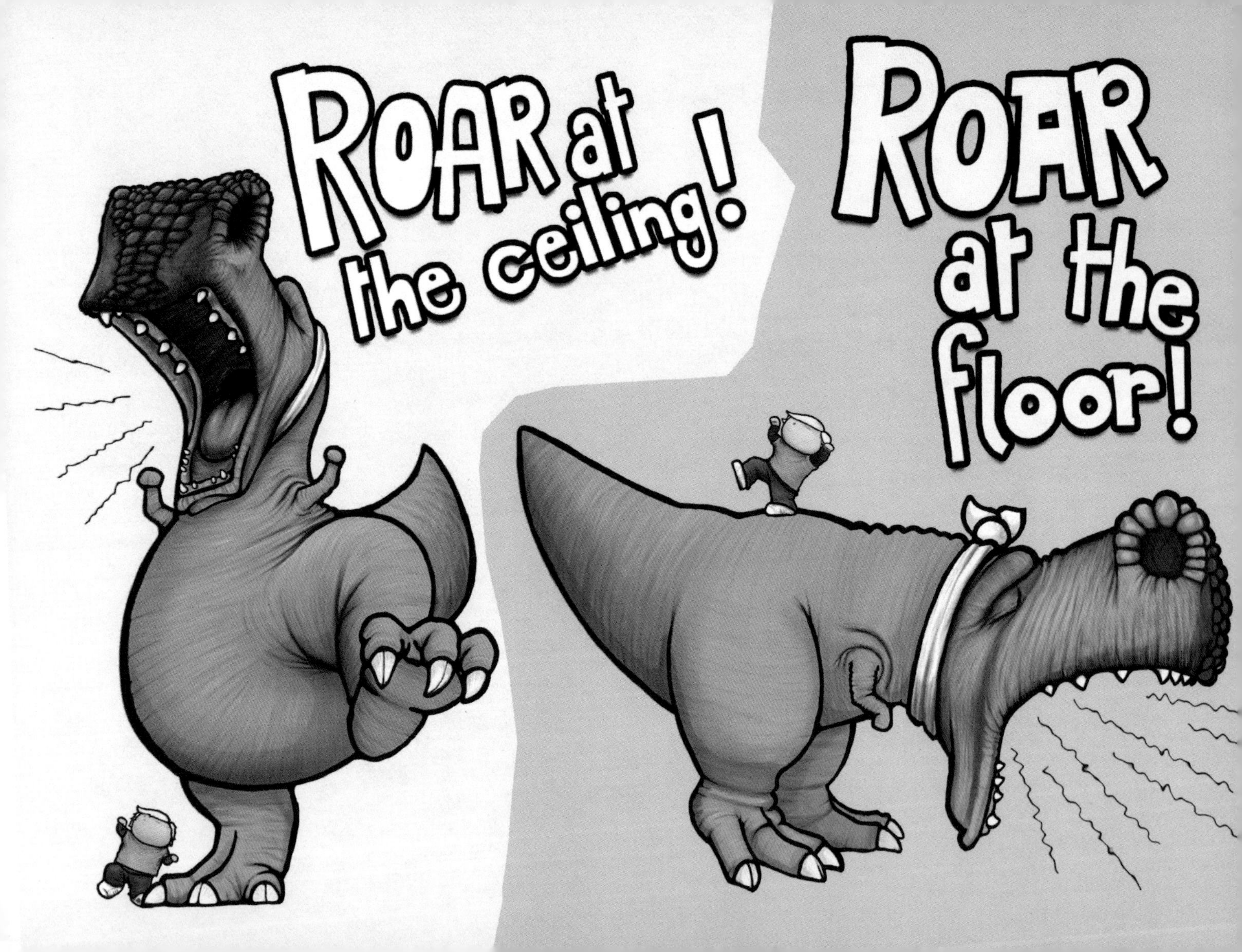
ROAR at the ceiling!
ROAR at the floor!

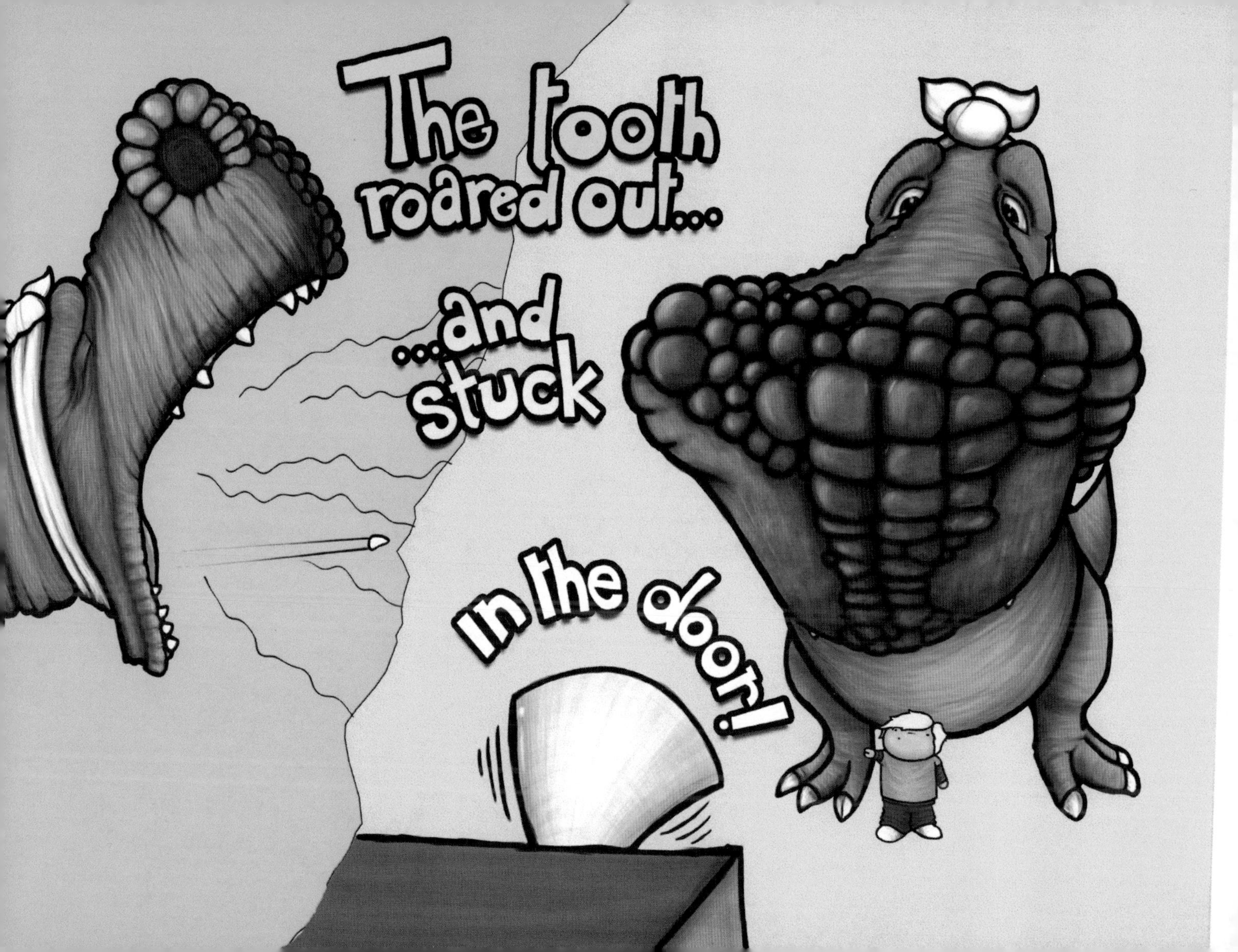
The tooth roared out...
...and stuck
in the door!

My T-Rex has
<u>no</u>
toothache,

he seems much more at ease.

But the only problem now is...
...my Pteranodon...

has a Sneeze!!!

54470269R00017

Made in the USA
Lexington, KY
16 August 2016